Animal Noises

By THOMAS FLINTHAM

SCHOLASTIC

The chickens wake the farm each day,
"CLUCK, CLUCK, CLUCK," the chickens say.

At breakfast time, the cows all chew,
In the meadow, "MOO, MOO, MOO".

The sheep all skip and jump up high,
"BAA!" these woolly farm friends cry.

The donkeys clip-clop through the door,
Calling out, "EEYORE, EEYORE".